"Let's go down there," Gaby whispered. She sat on the edge of the pit and slid down slowly, using her feet as anchors. When she got to the bottom, she stood up.

"Piece of cake!" she cried triumphantly.

Jasmine slid down next, and then Tina, cradling the camera in her lap. The three girls began to poke through the dirt. Tina found a large piece of old, dark-brown wood. She called the others to help her move it.

As they heaved at the heavy plank of wood, a glowing ball of light appeared in the air. It spun around their heads and circled the site three times. Suddenly it swooped down and disappeared underground. Ghost-writer! But Tina and Gaby were too busy to notice the arrival of their mysterious friend.

The piece of wood finally moved, and the girls gasped and stepped back. Half-buried in the dirt was a lump of yellow metal. Jasmine picked it up.

"What is it?" Tina asked.

"Is it *gold*?" Gaby breathed.

Join the Team!

Do you watch GHOSTWRITER on PBS? Then you know that when you read and write to solve a mystery or unravel a puzzle, you're using the same smarts and skills the Ghostwriter team uses.

We hope you'll join the team and read along to help solve the mysterious and puzzling goings-on in these GHOSTWRITER books!

A CHILDREN'S
TELEVISION
WORKSHOP BOOK

ghostwriter

DIGGING for CLUES

by
AMY KEYISHIAN
and
ELIZABETH KEYISHIAN

illustrated by
Phil Franké

BANTAM BOOKS
NEW YORK •
TORONTO •
LONDON •
SYDNEY •
AUCKLAND

DIGGING FOR CLUES
A Bantam Book / March 1994

Ghostwriter **Ghost**writer and

are trademarks of Children's Television Workshop.
All rights reserved. Used under authorization.

Art direction by Marva Martin
Cover design by Susan Herr
Interior illustrations by Phil Franké

ISBN 0-553-37262-9

Published simultaneously in the United States and Canada

Bantam Books are published by Bantam Books, a division of Bantam
Doubleday Dell Publishing Group, Inc. Its trademark, consisting of the
words "Bantam Books" and the portrayal of a rooster, is Registered in
U.S. Patent and Trademark Office and other countries. Marca Registrada.
Bantam Books, 1540 Broadway, New York, New York 10036.

PRINTED IN THE UNITED STATES OF AMERICA

OPM   0 9 8 7 6 5 4 3 2 1

Chapter 1

Usually, on Friday afternoons, Gaby Fernandez couldn't sit still. She would fidget on the front steps of Hurston Middle School till her brother, Alex, came out. But today she sat still, staring sadly at the blank notebook in her lap.

"Don't worry," her friend Tina Nguyen told her. "We'll think of something." Tina sat next to Gaby on the steps, holding a video camera.

"It has to be something *great*!" Gaby wailed. "This is a big contest." She pulled the flyer out of her notebook and unfolded it.

GO BACK! FIND HISTORY!

New York is full of history. Do you know where to find it? The Office of the Mayor of New York is holding a contest for all students. Find an example of history. Tell us how it still affects life today in the city. Your entry can be written, drawn, or videotaped.

1

"We could make a video that would win that contest," Tina said. "We just have to come up with the right idea. Let's keep thinking."

Gaby rested her chin on the edge of the notebook. Her eyes roamed up and down Myrtle Avenue. Then she sat up.

"I know!" she said. "How about 'Who named the streets of New York and why?' You know, like—who was Myrtle? Was the mayor in love with her? Did she break his heart? Or maybe Myrtle was his mother, who died in an epidemic. . . . "

"Well, the idea is good," Tina agreed, thinking. "But there are a lot of streets. How would we decide which ones to learn about? And I don't think we're going to find any stories of brokenhearted mayors."

"Oh, well." Gaby slumped down again.

"You could still write it down," Tina said. "Maybe it'll help us think of something else."

Gaby wrote in the notebook halfheartedly, then put her chin in her hand and stared out at the street. Almost immediately, she sat bolt upright again.

"This time I've really got it!" she cried. "We'll do a video project about when George Washington came to New York City and threw tea in the harbor, and fought the British, and invented Valentine's Day!"

"I don't think it happened that way," Tina said.

"Well, it sounded good," Gaby said.

Tina sighed. Gaby was energetic, but sometimes she could be sort of, well, scattered.

"Whoa!"

2

Tina felt someone stop behind her on the steps, and saw a notebook go sailing over her head. She looked up to see an older girl stooping to pick up her books. She was very pretty, with large dark eyes and glowing brown skin.

"I didn't see you guys there! I almost stepped on you. Sorry," the girl said.

"You're Jasmine, right? Jamal's gir— um, friend?" Gaby asked. She was very bold. Tina was already going to Hurston, yet often it seemed as if Gaby knew more Hurston students than she did.

"Yeah!" Jasmine said. "And you're Alex's sister. I'm in English class with him. He walks home with you, right? He should be right out—hey!" She pointed at the contest announcement. "Are you entering that? This could be fate. I've been trying to get someone to work with me on this great idea, but no one seems to have any time."

"Really? Well—what's your idea?" Tina asked.

"I live over in the projects, and they're putting up a supermarket in a vacant lot right nearby. They started construction, right? But when they started digging, they uncovered all this really neat old stuff."

"Old stuff?" Gaby's eyes were round with excitement.

"Yeah. Like *really* old. I don't even know what half of it could be. I thought it would be cool to collect a bunch of stuff from the construction site, then try to figure out where it came from."

"Hey, that would look great on video!" Tina

3

chimed in. "We have a video camera. Gaby borrowed it from Washington School. We were going to use it for the contest. We were looking for something to do a video project about!"

"That is so cool!" Jasmine said. "We could do a great project on video. I'll show you the stuff I already collected, then we can go down to the construction site."

Just then, Alex came up. "Hey, Gaby, hey, Tina," he said. "Jasmine, what's up? You know my sister?"

"We just met." Jasmine smiled. "Listen, Alex, can I borrow your sister for the afternoon? We just came up with the best idea for the city history contest."

"Well, she's supposed to help me work in the store—"

"Great! Thanks, Alex!" Gaby grabbed her notebook with one hand and Tina with the other, pulling her friend toward Jasmine. "I knew you'd understand! See you later!"

Gaby, Tina, and Jasmine were gone before Alex could say anything. He shook his head, muttering, and headed home.

"Here's where I live," Jasmine said. She pointed to a group of tall brown buildings. They walked through a courtyard to one of the buildings. Jasmine pulled a chain with a key from around her neck. She unlocked the heavy security door and pushed it open. Gaby and Tina followed her in. The lobby was crowded with people.

"I wonder what's going on," Jasmine said.

A young woman with light-brown skin and short, natural hair was speaking to the group. She was dressed in jeans and work boots with a red-and-green scarf around her neck.

"You all know me. From when I was a kid, I liked learning about our past. Right, Mrs. Roberts? Remember how I used to come up to your apartment and ask you about old buildings or old-fashioned signs, or the way people used to live around here?"

"That's right, Frieda. You sure did," an old woman called from the back. She had white hair and thick glasses. "I never heard so many questions!"

"You made me look at the neighborhood in a whole new way. To see the history behind all the new buildings. Now here I am, all grown up. And I still like to poke around this neighborhood, and find history here.

"I was down at the Shop-Mart construction site this morning and I found this." The young woman held up what looked like a thin white bone. "It's not much to look at, but to me, it's like finding gold."

People in the lobby jostled each other for a better view. The young woman smiled. "This is a piece of a pipe from the 1600s. Someone smoked this pipe three hundred years ago! Who was this person? What was it like back then? The answers are in that construction site. But they're waiting for us to dig them up. Maybe a family lived there. Someone who lives in these projects could be related to that family. We have no idea who

6

lived here, but we'd like you to help us find out!"

The crowd murmured, mostly in agreement.

"This is my partner, Ted." The woman gestured to a sandy-haired young man standing behind her. "He goes to school with me. We called a government agency named the Office of Historic Preservation—OHP for short—to ask them to stop this construction from going on. But the problem is, OHP will only stop construction if we prove this isn't just any old house from the 1600s. We have to show there's something special about this place. Something that will fill in some gaps in what we know about the past. Now, I have a feeling about this place. I *know* it's special. But a feeling isn't enough. We need proof. We'll find it by digging for it."

The young woman paused and took a deep breath. "And here's the catch. We only have this weekend to look. If we don't find anything, construction will start on Monday."

"Hold up, Frieda," a man in the lobby said. "Who cares if there's some old house buried in the ground? What do we want with it? This neighborhood needs a new supermarket! Not another ruin."

"I know that, Mr. Johnson," the young woman said. "I remember what it's like to live here. My mother still lives here. I know this neighborhood and what it needs. I promise the supermarket will get built. But first, we need the chance to dig up these clues to the past, before the bulldozers and jackhammers destroy them all!"

"What good does the past do us?" one woman asked.

"Would you ever have thought a farm sat on this land?" Frieda waved a hand at the door of the high-rise apartment building. "This isn't about soldiers or wars. It's about regular people who lived right here three hundred years ago. We need the chance to find out what we can about them."

People in the crowd began talking to each other. Mostly they sounded as if they agreed with Frieda. She and her partner looked at each other, happy.

"Can we count on volunteers to help us dig?" she asked.

"Yes!" the crowd shouted.

People began to cluster in small groups, talking excitedly about the new event in their neighborhood. Jasmine pulled Tina and Gaby toward the young woman.

"I'm Jasmine, and these are my friends Gaby and Tina. We're doing a video project on history in New York. Could we make our video about what you're doing at the site?"

"That would be fantastic!" Frieda beamed. "Ted!" she called to her partner. "We've already got TV coverage."

"Is this your job?" Gaby asked Frieda.

"Not exactly. We're graduate students at Columbia University. When we get our degrees, *then* we'll get paid for work like this. But for now, we do it for free." A group of people were waiting to talk to Frieda. "See you guys bright and early tomorrow morning, right?"

"I found a pipe just like what she found," Jasmine whispered after Frieda walked away. She drew a thin white object from her pocket and cupped it in her hands. Tina and Gaby stepped close to her, staring at it.

"The 1600s!" Tina said. "You're holding something that's more than three hundred years old." They all shivered. "I can't wait until tomorrow."

"I have a great idea," Gaby said with a big grin.

"Uh-oh. I know that look. Whatever you're thinking, I don't like it," Tina said. What was Gaby planning?

"What's your idea, Gaby?" Jasmine asked. She was grinning, too.

"You guys . . . " Tina objected.

"Let's go to the site now! We might find something excellent," Gaby said. "Come on, Tina!"

"Okay," Tina agreed. "But I have to be home by dinnertime."

"You will be!" Gaby said. "What could happen?"

Tina always worried when Gaby said things like that.

It was nearly dusk by the time the girls got to the vacant lot. The place was deserted. A few trailers were set up around the edges. Five or six huge construction machines sat around. They looked as if they were asleep. Signs all over the lot said BARRETT CONSTRUCTION. There was a huge pit in the middle of the open space.

"Is that where you found the pipe?" Gaby asked Jasmine.

"Yes," Jasmine replied. "When they made that hole, they uncovered all sorts of things."

"Let's go down there," Gaby whispered. She sat on the edge of the pit and slid down slowly, using her feet as anchors. When she got to the bottom, she stood up.

"Piece of cake!" she cried triumphantly.

Jasmine slid down next, and then Tina, cradling the camera in her lap. The three girls began to poke through the dirt. Tina found a large piece of old, dark-brown wood. She called the others to help her move it.

As they heaved at the heavy plank of wood, a glowing ball of light appeared in the air. It spun around their heads and circled the site three times. Suddenly it swooped down and disappeared underground. Ghostwriter! But Tina and Gaby were too busy to notice the arrival of their mysterious friend.

The piece of wood finally moved, and the girls gasped and stepped back. Half-buried in the dirt was a lump of yellow metal. Jasmine picked it up.

"What is it?" Tina asked.

"Is it *gold*?" Gaby breathed.

"I don't know," Jasmine answered both of them. She wiped away the dirt carefully with her shirttail.

The object was a few inches long, and it looked like a man's head. The man's eyes were closed, and he

seemed to have tattoos carved all over his face. He had many necklaces around his neck, too. The head was long and pointy.

"It looks African," Jasmine said. "Jamal's sister has a lot of African jewelry. This looks like some of it."

"Hey! *Hey!* You kids. What are you doing down there?" An angry voice interrupted their thoughts.

Tina, Gaby, and Jasmine looked up. A red-faced man in a suit stood at the edge of the pit. He began climbing down the side as they had, but wouldn't sit down to make himself go slowly. Dirt began to slide down with him. He waved his arms to steady himself and almost lost his balance. Gaby wanted to laugh, but she was too scared. Jasmine slipped the little metal head into her pocket.

Finally at the bottom, the man stormed over to them, wiping the dirt off his suit as he came.

"You are trespassing!" he shouted. "What are you doing here?"

"We were just—" Jasmine started, but the man cut in.

"I don't care what you were doing!" he yelled.

"Then why did you ask?" Gaby wanted to know.

"That's it!" The man's face turned purple. "You kids are in trouble. Big trouble!"

Chapter 2

"All of you, come with me!" The man began to walk toward one of the trailers. The girls looked at each other. Should they run away? The man turned around again.

"Come on. I want to talk to you!" He held open the door of the trailer.

Jasmine, Tina, and Gaby trooped inside and sat in a line on a musty, scratchy old couch. They looked around as the man paced up and down. There was a metal desk at one end of the room. It was cluttered with papers and folders. There were an old telephone and a lamp on it. There was also a nameplate that said TIMOTHY BARRETT. The walls were covered with maps of the site. An old ragged rug lay in the middle of the floor. At the far end of the trailer was a large built-in closet.

The man stopped pacing and glared at them. His cheeks were trembling. He sat down behind his desk.

"Now," he said, trying to remain calm. "What could you possibly have been looking for?"

"We were looking for history," Gaby said.

"We're making a history video," Tina added, holding up the camera.

Mr. Barrett's eyes got small and squinty. Suddenly he pounded his fist down on his desk. The girls jumped.

"*History?*" he scoffed. "There's no history here! Just progress! A nice new supermarket is going to be built here. Isn't that better than any dusty old history?"

Tina thought back to what Frieda had said. "We're not trying to stop you from building. We just want a chance to see what we can find first."

"There's nothing to find!" he shouted. Then he got very quiet and walked over to the couch, standing with his arms crossed. He looked at each of the girls in turn. "This is my construction site. You won't find anything here. I'll make sure of that."

He glared at them. They stared back, wide-eyed. No one knew what to say. Suddenly there was a knock at the door. Mr. Barrett looked up abruptly, and the girls sighed with relief. There was a second knock, this time louder.

"Hey! Are you in there, Barrett?" a good-natured voice called from outside.

Mr. Barrett opened the door and a smiling bald man with a mustache entered. Gaby remembered seeing him at Frieda's talk.

"Mr. Cruz!" Mr. Barrett growled, surprised. "I didn't think you were coming until tomorrow."

"I left OHP early today. I wanted to hear Frieda

14

and Ted speak to the neighborhood people. They've got a lot of volunteers. Everyone seems excited!"

"Yeah, well." Mr. Barrett smiled like a wolf. "Just remember, Shop-Mart didn't agree to stop construction. Today is Friday. We get to work on Monday. I don't know what you think they'll find in two days."

"We'll see." Mr. Cruz laughed. "They've got the whole weekend to look. Say, who are your friends here?"

"I think these are *your* friends," Mr. Barrett muttered. He turned back to the girls. "You can go now. Just don't forget what I said." He forced a thin smile onto his face.

The girls scrambled off the couch and out of the trailer before Mr. Barrett could change his mind. Mr. Cruz followed them out. Mr. Barrett stood in the doorway for a moment. Then he slammed the door shut.

Mr. Cruz turned to the girls.

"Phew!" he sighed. "He sure is cranky. I guess he doesn't like the idea of a lot of people crawling around his construction site this weekend."

"No kidding," Jasmine agreed. She introduced herself, Tina, and Gaby.

"We're making a video for a contest," Gaby added.

"Yeah. About history in New York," Tina said. "We thought it would be great to show how we can learn about early settlers by digging up what they left behind!"

"Oh, a documentary on archaeology!" Mr. Cruz said.

15

"Arky-what?" Gaby asked.

"Archaeology!" he repeated. "Archaeologists are scientists who study what other people leave behind."

"Really?" Gaby was fascinated.

"Yeah," Tina said. "Don't you remember when we went to see that Egyptian exhibit at the museum?"

Mr. Cruz nodded. "That's a good example. Someone had to go into the tombs of Egypt to find King Tut. That was an archaeologist. He looked at what the ancient Egyptians had left in the tomb. He also looked at their art, and other scientists figured out their language. That's how we know how they lived."

"I thought scientists wore white coats and worked with test tubes," Gaby said.

"That's just one kind of scientist," Mr. Cruz explained. "You met Frieda and Ted. They're studying to be archaeologists. They go to graduate school. That's where you keep going to school even after you've finished college, so you can learn as much as possible about one subject."

"Wow," Tina sighed.

"School *after* college?" Gaby's eyes widened. "They must really like studying that stuff."

"They do," Mr. Cruz agreed. "But I wish they had more time here," he added. "If they find anything important, we'll be able to pay for a real dig. We'll bring a whole team of archaeologists in and spend a few weeks studying the site." He glanced back at the trailer. "Anyway, I'll see you girls tomorrow."

"But—" Gaby started to say as he walked away. He

16

went over to a red car, unlocked it, and got in. He waved as he drove off. Gaby didn't have a chance to say what she was thinking. She wanted to tell him that Mr. Barrett had ordered them to stay away.

"Let's go," Tina asked. "It's starting to get dark."

"Okay," Gaby said. Then she stopped short. They could all hear Mr. Barrett yelling in his trailer. Gaby tiptoed back and put her ear against the door.

"I don't hear anyone else in there," she whispered to the other two. "So he must be on the phone. But I can't understand what he's saying."

Jasmine ran around to the back and beckoned to the other girls. There was a small vent near the top of the trailer. Jasmine and Tina crouched down and Gaby stepped onto their shoulders. They stood up carefully.

Balanced on their shoulders, Gaby was much closer to the vent. She listened to the conversation inside.

"I've got to get them out of here!" Barrett was yelling angrily. "This place will be crawling with people all weekend. If they find anything, that government agency will force us to close while they dig up the whole site!"

He paused while the other person spoke.

"No, I *can't* just be patient! The Shop-Mart Company pays me to oversee construction. I get paid a bonus if it gets done on time and on budget. I want that extra money!" He paused again, then sighed.

"Fine. I'll do it without your help. I'll make sure this job isn't held up by some stupid history buffs!"

Gaby gasped. Mr. Barrett wanted to stop the stu-

dent dig! She twisted around and began whispering what she had heard to the others.

"Who's out there?" Mr. Barrett thundered.

He must have heard them whispering! Gaby tried to climb off Jasmine and Tina's shoulders, but they were both already trying to run. Tina ran toward Jasmine. Jasmine ran toward Tina. Gaby fell on top of both of them. All three girls landed in a confused heap. They were still trying to untangle themselves when Mr. Barrett came around the corner.

He loomed over them. He looked even bigger and meaner in the twilight.

"I told you kids to clear out!" he yelled.

Tina and Jasmine were too frightened to answer. They looked at Gaby. But for once, she was speechless, too.

Chapter 3

"Mr. Barrett!" Tina gasped. "We were just— We wanted to interview you!"

"Interview me?" Mr. Barrett was taken aback.

"Yeah! For our documentary—for the project!" Tina turned on the camera and pointed it at Mr. Barrett.

"I—uh—" Mr. Barrett stammered.

Gaby got up quickly and stood next to him, looking at the camera.

"Do you think history is important?" she asked him.

He looked at her, confused. "What?"

"What's the matter?" Gaby asked. "Don't you want to be interviewed right now?"

"No. No, I don't!" He looked suspiciously at all three of them again. "Forget it. Just—just get out of here! All of you, now!"

The girls didn't need to be asked twice. Tina shut off the camera. "Maybe another time," she said politely.

Then the girls walked away, calmly but quickly.

As soon as they turned the corner, all three broke into a run. They ran two blocks together, giggling, then stopped, out of breath. "This is where I go home," Jasmine said, still laughing. "You guys were great under pressure."

Tina smiled. "This will win the prize for sure!"

"*If* Mr. Barrett will let us find anything," Gaby said.

"He's just full of hot air," Jasmine said.

"He said he would *make sure* we didn't find anything. I'll bet he'll do anything to keep us away from there!"

"Gaby!" Tina rolled her eyes.

"No, really! I'll bet he's planning to mess up Frieda's dig! He might wreck everything."

"How could he wreck everything?" Tina asked.

"I don't know! He might hire security guards to stop us from going to the construction site. Or maybe he'll get some big dogs, and set them loose on us when we're working there! Or maybe—"

"Gaby," Jasmine interrupted. "You've been watching too many spy movies. It's like Mr. Cruz said, Mr. Barrett is just a cranky guy."

"I'm telling you guys! Really! I'm sure he's going to try something!" Gaby protested.

"Well, maybe," Tina said. "But if I don't get home soon, Mr. Barrett will look like a pussycat next to my father. He hates it when I'm late!"

"We'll meet tomorrow at the site, okay?" Jasmine asked.

"Okay!" Gaby and Tina answered.

By the time Tina got home, she was already late for dinner. She sighed, knowing she'd be in trouble when she got inside. She opened the door quietly and went in.

Her whole family was already sitting at the table: her mother, her father, her older brother, Tuan, and her little sister, Linda. The food was on their plates, steaming. But something was wrong. No one looked at her when she walked in. They didn't even seem to notice she was late!

"Sorry I'm late," she whispered, sliding into her seat next to Linda. But still no one seemed to hear her. She glanced at Linda. Linda was staring at their father. Tina looked at him. He was glaring at Tuan, who was looking down at his food. A heavy silence hung over the table.

"What kind of a thing is this to say?" Mr. Nguyen growled at Tuan. "Hmm? What are you saying to me?"

Tuan looked at his father. "I would like to move out," he said. "I think it would be best for all of us."

"What's best for all of us is my decision!"

"I can't stay here forever, you know. I'm going to be out of high school soon. I'm an adult," Tuan answered.

"An adult? What does that mean? I am still your

father! You do not live outside of this house until I tell you it is right!"

"You'd like it if I lived here forever!" Tuan yelled.

"Please, please, both of you." Mrs. Nguyen's voice was quavery with fear and sorrow. She hated it when the family argued. "Tuan, what about your school? Don't you want to keep studying, so you can go to college?"

"Of course," Tuan said. "But I can't live here. Especially not when I get to college. I need my own space!"

Tina felt her stomach clench up. Why did Tuan say such things? Sometimes she thought he did it on purpose just to make Father angry.

"I'm a musician," Tuan went on. "I'm going to stay with Dave from the band for the weekend. If I like it, he says I can move in with him. I'll get a job to pay the rent. I'm not asking you for anything. I'm just letting you know what I'm doing."

"You're letting me know," Tina's father said quietly. Then he began shouting again. "You do not let me know! I let you know! And I am letting you know right now that you are not moving out of this house to go and live with some crazy musicians playing the rock and roll with the hair and rings in the ears and girls all over the place! You are living right here and learning to respect your family!" He was standing now, hands on the table, leaning toward Tuan. "When I was your age I was working in my cousin's tailor shop! Not playing some guitar! I did not insult my family with craziness about moving out!"

Linda began to sniffle. She was only six, and sometimes she didn't understand everything that went on. Tina moved closer to her and put her arm around her.

"Dad, this isn't Saigon," Tuan began.

"No! This is *not* Saigon! This is America! Do you know why you are in America now? Because I worked to bring you here! I am your father! And you do not 'let me know' you're moving out!"

Tuan stood up. "I have to live my life now. I can't stay in this house!" He stormed out the door.

Mr. Nguyen followed him. "Don't walk away from me! What I am saying, goes! You always think you know best, but I know best!"

Linda finally burst into loud tears and ran to her room.

"Where is she going?" Mr. Nguyen shouted, turning back to the table. "Linda, get back here! We are having dinner!"

Mrs. Nguyen got up and went after Linda.

"Where are you going now?" Mr. Nguyen asked.

His wife looked at him sadly and left the kitchen.

The fire seemed to have gone out of Tina's father's eyes. He suddenly looked very old. He sat down. Tina was the only person left at the table with him.

"I'll have some dinner with you, Father," Tina offered. He looked up slowly. She moved her chair closer to his.

"The food is cold," he said.

"The noodles are still warm. They were covered up. Do you want some?" she asked. He nodded.

They ate together in silence.

Later, Tina was in the bedroom she shared with Linda. She could hear her parents arguing quietly in their room. The apartment seemed lonely, even though it was full of people. Tina switched on a lamp. Then she reached under her bed and got out her secret box. Inside were some pictures and her lucky charm, an old-fashioned subway token with a "Y" stamped through the middle of it. There was also a spiral-bound note-book with DIARY written in script across the front. She opened it and began to write.

Dear Diary:

Everything seems to be turned upside down in my house. I used to think that my home was the safest place in the world. I also used to think everything would always stay the same. Now I wonder. Everything in my life could change at any time! I don't just mean my brother moving out. My father got so upset. He started talking about when he was young, in Vietnam. He never thought he would have to leave his home, but he had to make the journey all the way here, to America. He must have been scared! And he must have felt sad to leave his home!

26

Tina thought for a minute, then kept writing.

> What if I had to leave my home and go somewhere strange, the way my father did? I would be so scared. Is everything going to be okay?

Tina closed her eyes and leaned back against the wall for a moment. Then she looked back at the page. What she saw made her gasp. A sparkling, glowing light was moving back and forth over her page of writing.

"Ghostwriter!" she said. Her sister turned over in her sleep. Tina held her breath and looked at her, but Linda didn't wake up.

Ghostwriter was a mysterious friend of Tina, Gaby, and the rest of the Ghostwriter Team—Jamal, Lenni, Rob, and Gaby's brother, Alex. All they knew about him was that he was a ghost, but not a scary one. He could communicate with them only by reading and writing. He could read anything, and could write back to them. He was their friend, and they knew they could always count on him.

Suddenly the words Tina had been writing rearranged themselves into something else.

> WILL MY FAMILY BE ALL RIGHT? I AM SO SCARED AND SAD! I WISH SOMEONE WOULD COMFORT ME! BUT MY YOUNGER BROTHERS AND SISTERS NEED MORE COMFORT THAN I DO. I HAVE TO THINK OF THEM AND BE STRONG.

Tina read all of this, puzzled. Then she wrote back:

GHOSTWRITER? DID YOU WRITE THIS?

I READ IT. SOMEONE ELSE IS FEELING THE WAY YOU ARE.

CAN YOU SHOW ME SOME MORE OF WHAT THIS PERSON WROTE?

IT'S HARD TO READ. THE WRITING IS VERY FADED. I FOUND THIS NEARBY: MAARTJE SALEE, 11 YEARS OLD.

My age! thought Tina.

WHO IS SHE? she scribbled in her diary.

I DON'T KNOW. I'LL LOOK FOR SOMETHING ELSE SHE WROTE.

OKAY. THANKS, GHOSTWRITER!

Tina glanced at the clock. Nine-thirty. It was still early enough to call Gaby. She tiptoed out to the kitchen phone and dialed Gaby's number. Gaby answered.

"What's up, Tina?" she asked.

"Guess what just happened!" Tina said. "Ghost-writer found some girl's diary. I think she's in trouble!"

"Someone else's diary? Whose?"

"I don't know who she is, but she's really upset about something. Her name is Maartje."

"Mart-juh?" Gaby echoed. "What kind of name is that?"

"I don't know—maybe she's from some other country. Do you know anyone named Maartje?"

"No . . . there's Martha . . . "

"No. It's definitely Maartje. Maartje Salee."

Tina heard her parents walking around the bedroom. She didn't want them to come out and see her on the telephone. They might get angry at her, too.

"I have to go, Gaby!"

"All right. Come over first thing after breakfast tomorrow. We'll figure out who she is."

"And we'll help her, right?"

"Right! Bye."

"Bye, Gaby." Tina hung up. Then she went back to her room. She was thinking hard. Who was Maartje? And what was happening to her right now?

Chapter 4

By the time Tina got to Gaby's house, she felt nervous and sad all over again. No one had spoken to anyone else all through breakfast. But I can't worry about that now! she said to herself. Gaby and I have to figure out what is going on with this mysterious girl, Maartje. And we have to plan this video! She walked through Gaby's parents' bodega to the back, and knocked on their apartment door.

"Hi, Tina!" Gaby was cheerful. "Come on in." Tina stepped into the kitchen and smiled. Gaby frowned.

"Hey, is everything okay?" she asked. "You look kind of tired or something."

Tina didn't want to think about the trouble at home anymore. If she talked about it to Gaby, she would have to think about it. She smiled. "It's nothing."

"Well, okay." Gaby didn't sound convinced. "But if there is anything, I hope you'll tell me." Tina followed Gaby to the bedroom she shared with Alex, where the rest of the Ghostwriter Team was already sitting.

Jamal Jenkins was by the window. On the end of Gaby's bed sat Lenni Frazier, and next to her was Rob Baker. Gaby's brother, Alex, sat on the floor. Gaby always talked about what a pain Alex was, but Tina liked him a lot. She had even gone to the movies with him once. She smiled at him. When he smiled back, her heart skipped a little.

All the kids wore black pens around their necks, especially for writing to Ghostwriter.

"What's everyone doing here?" Tina asked. "Did someone call a rally?"

"I did," said Gaby. "It sounded important, and I thought six heads were better than one."

"What's this mysterious message you got last night?" Alex prodded.

Tina told the team about Ghostwriter's message from Maartje's diary. "She seems really upset," Tina concluded. "I want to find her and help her."

"That's pretty wild," Alex said. He looked at Gaby. "For once you're not freaking out over nothing!"

Gaby scowled. Alex really knew how to get under her skin. "If you're not going to help, then just forget it!"

"Of course he'll help," Lenni said, kicking Alex. She knew that if he and Gaby got into a fight, she'd never hear the story. "We all will."

"What can we do?" Rob asked.

"Maybe we should write down everything we know about Maartje," Jamal said.

Gaby opened a loose-leaf notebook. Across the front, she had written CASEBOOK. "Well, we know her name, for starters." She wrote: "Maartje Salee."

"And we know how old she is. Eleven," Tina said. Gaby wrote that down, too.

"We know that she's sad, and that something bad is happening to her family," Alex said, and Gaby wrote that down, too. The six kids were quiet for a moment, looking at the list.

MAARTJE SALEE
ELEVEN YEARS OLD
REALLY SAD
SOMETHING BAD IS HAPPENING TO FAMILY

"That's about all we know," Tina said, sighing.

"I really want to find out more," Lenni said. "But the thing is, we're already late for the meeting with the school advisers about our writing the big spring show at Hurston. If we miss this meeting, there won't be a show!" She turned to Gaby and Tina. "Can you guys do it without us, for now?"

"And let us know the second anything happens," Rob added.

"We can handle it," Gaby assured them. "For now. But you'd all better be there when we call the next rally!"

"Of course," Jamal said.

Lenni, Jamal, Alex, and Rob left the apartment, running so they would get to Hurston in time for the meeting. Tina and Gaby looked at each other.

"Maybe there's nothing else to find out," Gaby said.

"There's got to be!" Tina snapped. Gaby looked surprised. "I'm sorry," Tina said. "I just feel like . . . like if I were feeling the way Maartje is, I would want to know people were on my side."

"Okay," Gaby agreed. "Well, I know one place we can look for clues."

"Where?" Tina asked.

"Right here!" Gaby answered, triumphant. She began to write in her notebook:

"Ghostwriter, have you found out anything else about Maartje?"

A glowing yellow light moved over the words on page. Then more of Ghostwriter's writing appeared.

I CANNOT FIND THE BRONZE PENDANT PAPA GAVE ME. HE BROUGHT IT WITH HIM WHEN HE CAME HERE FROM THE BIGHT OF BENIN. IT IS MY MOST PRIZED POSSESSION, AND NOW PAPA SAYS I DON'T HAVE TIME TO EVEN LOOK FOR IT. WE MUST LEAVE.

The writing stopped. Gaby and Tina looked at the page, then at each other.

"What is she talking about?" Gaby asked.

"Well . . ." Tina thought for a minute. "She lost something. And now she can't find it, because she has to leave right away. Her family is in some kind of hurry."

Just then, Ghostwriter returned. They watched as more words formed on the page.

HE SAYS THAT THE RED COATS ARE TAKING OVER THIS AREA. IT'S SO DARK. I WISH I WERE ASLEEP IN MY BED. BUT I'LL PROBABLY NEVER SEE MY BED AGAIN. AM MISERABLE. I WISH I WERE DEAD.

Tina and Gaby looked at each other. This was worse than they had thought!

Gaby quickly wrote the new clues underneath what they already knew about Maartje.

"She lost something very precious. A pendant from the Bight of Benin." Gaby looked up. "What's a Bight of Benin?"

"I don't know. Write it down, and we'll look it up later," Tina directed. Gaby nodded and kept writing.

"And . . ." Tina continued, then stopped.

"What is it?" Gaby asked.

"Well, she says they have an enemy, the red coats. Who are the red coats?"

"Maybe it's a *gang*!" Gaby breathed. "I saw this movie once where there was a gang and they all wore black hats and white suits. They went around wrecking people's lives. Maybe these guys wear red, and they are going to come and wreck Maartje's house!"

34

"I don't know," Tina said. "I never heard of a gang like that in real life. Come on, let's go to the library and start looking this stuff up."

Gaby pouted. "The library? But that will take so long. Can't we just figure it out *now*?"

"I don't think we can figure it out ourselves. Do you?" Tina wanted to know. Gaby took out a pen and started writing.

GHOSTWRITER! DO YOU KNOW ANYTHING ABOUT THE BIGHT OF BENIN?

SORRY. I CAN'T HELP YOU. HAVE YOU THOUGHT OF GOING TO THE LIBRARY?

Gaby laughed. "Good idea, Ghostwriter. I wish I'd thought of it myself."

The girls took the subway to the library. It was a huge building with about a million steps leading up to it. It had big, tall windows and gold-colored pictures running across the front. Tina and Gaby went in and looked at the map on the wall to the right.

"We want the reference department," Tina said. "It's on the second floor." They went up the escalator and into a huge room. Not only were the walls covered with books, there were bookshelves running up and down the middle of the room, too.

"Whoa," Gaby said. "Where do we start?"

"If we needed help, we'd ask the librarian," Tina said. "But I think we can start right here." On one of the tables in the room, there were already some books set out. Tina opened one that said ATLAS.

"This is a book of maps," she said. "We can find

any place in the world in it." She turned to the back and began looking through the index. "Aha!"

"Aha?" Gaby asked. "What did you find?"

"Benin is a country in Africa," Tina said, pointing.

"Africa?" Gaby shook her head. "So Maartje's father came from Africa?"

"I guess so."

"Well, then—where is the Bight of Benin?" Gaby asked.

"I don't know," Tina said. She looked through the atlas some more, but it didn't tell them what a Bight was.

"Let's look in the dictionary." Gaby pulled another of the big books toward them. She flipped through the pages.

"Aha again!" she said. "Bight is another word for Bay. The Bight of Benin is the Bay of Benin." They looked at the map of Africa. In the country of Benin, there was a dent where the ocean poked into the land a little bit. Gaby traced her finger along the dent.

"So Maartje's father came from right here," she whispered. "Cool."

"Maybe we can find out more from the encyclopedia," Tina said. She and Gaby went to one of the shelves along the wall. Tina found Volume "B" of the encyclopedia and pulled it off the shelf. They took it back to the table and opened it to the entry for Benin.

"Well, it says Benin used to be called Dahomey. And it was famous for bronze sculpture from the 1400s to the 1600s," Gaby read.

37

"Great. Do you see any information that helps us *now?*"

"Not really. It doesn't say anything about people who came to America from Benin. And it doesn't mention Maartje's family."

"Well, at least we know where her family is from," Tina said. "But we still don't know who she is. Maybe if we could get her address, we could go watch and see if someone suspicious is hanging around there. Come on."

Tina led Gaby to a telephone booth on the ground floor.

"Are we going to call someone?" Gaby asked.

Tina reached under the telephone and pulled out the Brooklyn phone book. "We know Maartje's last name," she said. "Maybe she's in here."

Tina flipped through the telephone book, but when she got to the letter "S," she let out a groan.

"What's the matter?" Gaby asked.

"Take a look," Tina said.

There were at least fifteen people with the last name Salee in the phone book.

"Well, should we call them all?" Gaby wondered.

"No way. I don't have that many quarters," Tina said firmly. "And there's no guarantee she's at any of these addresses. This is a dead end."

"Tina, wait," Gaby said. "I have an idea."

Gaby sat on the steps outside the phone booth. She opened her casebook and started writing.

38

GHOSTWRITER?

The glowing light appeared almost immediately. It passed over the letters in his name, then made them light up. Tina smiled as Gaby kept writing.

PLEASE LOOK IN HURSTON'S SCHOOL RECORDS. FIND MAARTJE SALEE. IF SHE'S ELEVEN YEARS OLD, SHE'S PROBABLY IN THE SIXTH GRADE. WE NEED HER ADDRESS.

Ghostwriter read the words, then disappeared. But he didn't come back right away, the way he usually did.

What's taking so long? Gaby wondered.

They sat there for several more minutes, staring at the page. Finally Ghostwriter returned.

I'M SORRY. THERE'S NO MAARTJE SALEE IN EITHER OF YOUR SCHOOLS. I CAN'T FIND HER IN ALL OF BROOKLYN!

"She's not in the school records," Tina said and began writing again.

THANKS ANYWAY, GHOSTWRITER.

"That means we only have her diary to use as clues," Gaby said. "It's not enough. We can't find anything out!"

"I know," Tina said. "Maybe we can't help her at all." She felt frustrated and sad. She took out her pen and wrote at the bottom of the page:

"WHERE ARE YOU, MAARTJE?"

But there was no answer.

Chapter 5

Gaby looked at her watch. "Whoops," she said.

"Shhhh!" a lady at the next table said.

"Whoops," Gaby whispered. "We're supposed to meet Jasmine at the construction site. We're really late!"

"I think we've found out everything we could about Maartje here, anyway," Tina said, closing the casebook.

"We should be able to get some great stuff for the video today," Gaby observed as they walked out of the library.

"The video! I left the camera at my house," Tina said.

"We'll stop there on our way to the site," Gaby suggested.

"Oh, you don't have to come—I mean—if you want to go straight to the site, I can meet you there . . ."

"What are you talking about? It will take five seconds. Come on, we'll hurry." Gaby was already headed down into the subway. Tina sighed and followed her.

When they got to Tina's house, Mr. Nguyen was at the kitchen table, reading a Vietnamese newspaper. Tina looked around anxiously, but everything seemed pretty normal.

"Hello, Gaby." Mr. Nguyen looked up and smiled.

"Hi, Mr. Nguyen."

Just then, Tuan came into the apartment with one of the guys from his band.

"I'm here to get my stuff," he said.

Mr. Nguyen smiled at Tuan's friend.

"It is very nice to see you, David," he said. "But I must inform you that Tuan is not moving in with you. He is staying here, with his family."

"I'm not!" Tuan shouted. He walked past his father to the corner of the living room where he slept. He slammed open the dresser that held his clothes. Tina could hear him stomping around, throwing things into his duffel bag. Dave looked uncomfortable. Mr. Nguyen stood up and went over to his son.

"What do you think you are doing? I said you are staying here!" he shouted in Vietnamese.

"Talk English, Father. I told you I'm moving out."

Tuan came out into the kitchen. "Let's go," he said to David as he pushed past Tina and went out the door. David shrugged and followed him out. Mr. Nguyen looked out after them, then sat heavily down at the table. Tina could hear her mother crying softly in her parents' bedroom.

"I'll get the camera," she whispered, her face burning with embarrassment.

41

Gaby watched her friend carefully as they left Tina's apartment building. "Are you okay?" she asked.

"Sure. It was just a dumb argument. It doesn't mean anything's going to happen. It doesn't mean the family is falling apart or anything. Everything is fine." Tina stopped walking and looked at Gaby helplessly.

"Well, maybe it's not *fine*," Gaby said, putting her arm around her friend's shoulders. "But you can always talk to me about it."

"Thanks, Gaby," Tina said. But she didn't say anything else. They kept walking.

When they got to the site, Jasmine ran up to them. "Where have you guys been? So much has been happening!" she said enthusiastically.

Gaby and Tina looked around them. The vacant lot they had seen the day before had been replaced by a humming outdoor workshop. The whole area was broken up into three-foot squares, marked by long pieces of string tied to little wooden pegs in the ground. In each square, three or four people were scraping carefully away at the dirt. Along one side of the construction site, big screens were lying on top of wooden dividers while people poured water over them. Everyone looked very busy.

Gaby glanced over at Mr. Barrett's trailer. It was locked up. There was no sign of him.

"Isn't that cool?" Jasmine pointed to the screens.

"What are they doing?" Tina asked, hoisting the

42

camera to her shoulder and beginning to tape. They walked over to get a better look.

"Whenever they think they've found something that isn't too delicate to handle, they bring it over here," Jasmine explained. "They run the water over it to get rid of the dirt. The water and dirt go through the screen, and the artifact stays on top where you can see it!"

"Artifact?" Gaby repeated.

"That's the scientific name for all the old stuff we found here. Frieda will tell you about it. Hey, Frieda!"

"Hi, Tina and Gaby," Frieda said, walking up. "You guys ready to roll? I'm ready to be part of history!"

Tina turned the camera toward her, and Gaby took her post at her side as the reporter.

Through the camera lens, Tina framed Frieda and some of the volunteer diggers behind her. In the background of her shot, a red-faced man scowled at her. Mr. Barrett! Tina looked up from the camera, but he had disappeared.

"Ready, Tina?" Gaby asked. Tina nodded.

"What have you found out so far?" Gaby asked Frieda.

"Well, first of all," Frieda said, walking along the row of screens, "we know this was a farmhouse."

"A farmhouse? In Brooklyn?" Gaby was stunned.

"This was all farmland at one time," Frieda said. "The house is probably from the late 1600s. Brooklyn was founded by the Dutch, you know. They named it. They called it Breukelen, or 'Broken Land.' "

"Why 'broken land'?" Gaby wanted to know.

"It was named after a place in Holland, where they came from," Frieda answered. "Anyway, the first European settlers in this whole area—Brooklyn and Manhattan—were the Dutch. A lot of places in New York have Dutch names—Amsterdam Avenue, the Holland Tunnel. The first governor of the area was a Dutchman named Peter Stuyvesant."

"Like Stuyvesant High and Stuyvesant Park?" Tina asked.

"That's right. Anyway, in 1664, settlers from England began taking over the area. We think this farmhouse belonged to Dutch settlers who were forced to leave."

Jasmine, Tina, and Gaby looked around them. 1664! That was really a long time ago.

"Anyway," Frieda continued, "everything we find here is a clue. And every clue brings us one step closer to figuring out the whole story of this place."

Jasmine gasped. "That reminds me! I forgot to give this to you. I found it here yesterday." She drew the yellow statue from her pocket. "We thought it looked African, but maybe it's Dutch."

"No way. This is African." Frieda studied the little head. She seemed very excited all of a sudden. "Ted has studied a lot of African stuff. Hey! Ted, come over here!"

They were joined by the quiet young man. "Jasmine found this here yesterday," Frieda said, handing it to him.

He cradled the little head in his hands. "This is fantastic," he said. "It looks like bronze. It's typical of the style of Western Africa, probably from around the Bight of Benin. It's very old—and very valuable. Boy, if we could find more stuff like this, that would really help us prove this site is unique."

"That's what I was thinking," Frieda said. She turned back to the girls. "Where exactly did you find this?"

"Under a piece of wood in the big pit that the construction workers dug," Gaby said. Her mind was racing. She looked at Tina, but didn't say anything. Tina had stopped taping. She looked as if her eyes were going to pop out of her head. They were both thinking the same thing. Mentally, Gaby ran down a list in her head: Bronze . . . Bight of Benin . . . Africa . . .

This little object must be the pendant Maartje had been talking about in her diary!

But what was Maartje's pendant doing here, buried at this construction site?

Chapter
6

As soon as they could, Gaby and Tina walked away from Jasmine, Frieda, and Ted. They began talking in excited whispers.

"So Maartje's pendant somehow ended up at this construction site," Gaby said. "But how did it get here? Did she hide it?"

"It took three of us to move that big board," Tina pointed out. "She couldn't have hidden it there herself. Could she?"

"I don't know!" Gaby put her hands on her head. She felt as if it might explode with all the new facts buzzing around in it. "Maybe we should ask Frieda and Ted."

"We can't tell anyone about Ghostwriter," Tina said. "What would we say? That we have a hunch that someone might have written in her diary about that pendant?"

"You're right," Gaby said. "There's only one thing to do."

Gaby and Tina looked at each other and smiled. "Rally!" they said at the same time.

Gaby pulled a sheet of paper from her notebook. RALLY—G! she wrote.

At the Youth Center, Jamal was playing a video game against Momo. He was winning. His Ninja warrior was backing Momo's Marine against a brick wall. Suddenly the words at the bottom of the screen began rearranging themselves. They met in the middle of the screen to say, "RALLY—G!" Jamal stopped for a second, reading. Momo immediately began tapping his controller at top speed. His Marine began kicking Jamal's Ninja across the screen.

"I just remembered," Jamal said. "There's something I've got to do!"

"Yo, man, what about the game? You going to quit just when I start winning?" Momo said.

"Sorry. Victor, take over." Jamal gave his controller to Victor Torres, a friend of Rob's. Momo sighed. Victor was even better at this game than Jamal!

Jamal ran out the door of the Youth Center at top speed, on his way to Gaby and Alex's house.

Lenni and Alex were in Lenni's loft.

"Alex," Lenni grumbled. "We're supposed to be working on the spring musical. Why are you watching that stupid game show?"

"I never get to watch it!" Alex protested. "Come

47

on, Lenni. Just this one show, then I promise we'll work."

"What's so great about it, anyway?" Lenni asked, sitting next to him. "They just unscramble words. It's boring!"

As Lenni and Alex looked at the TV screen, one of the scrambled words began to glow and pulsate.

"Whoa—do you see what I see?" Alex said.

"Looks like Ghostwriter!" Lenni confirmed. The letters moved to the bottom of the screen to spell out, "RALLY—G!"

"Let's go!" Lenni said, moving to the door.

"Man, I *never* get to watch this show," Alex grumbled, following her.

"Rob!" Mrs. Baker yelled from the other end of their apartment. "Get off that phone now. You'll be seeing your brother in a few weeks when he comes home for the summer!"

"All right, Mom, just two more minutes," Rob called back. He continued typing into the small box attached to the phone.

"Mom wants me to get off the phone," he wrote. The words were sent over the phone line to a similar box near the phone of his brother, Jason, who was at a boarding school for the deaf.

"What do you expect?" his brother's message came back. "We've been talking for over an hour." Suddenly the letters on the box began to dance around.

"Jason?" Rob said out loud. Then he realized—Ghostwriter was trying to contact him.

"RALLY—G!" the letters now said.

"Jason, buddy, I gotta go," he typed in.

"Okay, man. See you in a couple weeks. Meanwhile, you'd better write back!"

"I promise. Bye!" Rob typed in hastily, then grabbed his jeans jacket and headed for the door. "I'm off the phone, Mom!" he called just as the door closed behind him.

Rob was the last to arrive at the Fernandez apartment. He hurried into Gaby and Alex's room and threw himself on Alex's bed. "Okay! I'm here. What's up?" he asked.

Lenni passed him the casebook. "Tina and Gaby are into a serious mystery, and we've been missing it!" she said.

"Remember how Ghostwriter found pieces of a diary about a girl who's really lonely and scared?" Jamal asked.

"Yeah, I remember," Rob said.

"Well, Jasmine found the pendant that the girl said she lost. It was in the vacant lot where they're digging up that old farmhouse! Somehow this girl Maartje is connected with the archaeological dig. But we don't know how!"

"We thought it was time the whole team got involved," Tina said. She began to write. GHOSTWRITER,

49

EVERYONE IS HERE. DID YOU FIND ANY MORE OF MAARTJE'S DIARY?

In answer, writing began to appear.

PAPA WAS FRIGHTENING ME BEFORE. HE WAS SHOUTING AT EACH OF US TO DO A DIFFERENT JOB: PACK OUR BELONGINGS INTO TRUNKS, LASH THE TRUNKS ONTO OUR WAGON, GET FOOD READY FOR OUR TRIP. THE TIME HAS COME TO LEAVE OUR HOME FOREVER. I HAVE DECIDED TO LEAVE THESE WRIT-INGS BEHIND, AS A WAY TO LEAVE PART OF MYSELF HERE.

The writing stopped abruptly. The Ghostwriter Team stared at the page for a moment.

IS THIS THE END? Tina wrote.

A moment passed before Ghostwriter replied, THIS ENTRY STOPS HERE, BUT THERE IS ANOTHER ONE NEARBY. After a few more seconds, the writing continued.

PAPA JUST CAME OVER AND RESTED HIS HEAD AGAINST MINE. "I'M SORRY, MAARTJE," HE SAID. "I KNOW THIS SEEMS STRANGE TO YOU. BUT WE CAN'T STAY HERE WHEN THE RED COATS TAKE OVER." HE FEARED THAT THE RED COATS WILL ABUSE US, SIM-PLY BECAUSE OUR FATHER COMES FROM AFRICA. HE ALSO SAYS THAT THEY MAY NOT ALLOW MAMA TO

STAY WITH PAPA BECAUSE SHE IS DUTCH AND HER
SKIN IS WHITE. I DON'T UNDERSTAND.

"Wait. Her mother is Dutch?" Rob asked.

"I guess so," Alex said. "Her mother is Dutch, her
father is African, and somebody thinks they shouldn't
be together. Wow, this is serious!"

"Here comes some more writing," Tina said.

THESE RED COATS ARE STRANGE PEOPLE. I ASKED
PAPA WHY IT WAS SO IMPORTANT FOR ME TO LEARN
THEIR LANGUAGE. HE SAID IT WOULD HELP ME IF
EVER I AM FORCED TO LIVE AMONG THEM.
STRANGE. WHEN HE FIRST TAUGHT ME THIS LAN-
GUAGE, I THOUGHT OF IT AS A SECRET LANGUAGE
JUST FOR ME. BUT SOMEDAY MY VERY LIFE MAY DE-
PEND ON IT. WE ARE GOING NOW. IF ANYONE
READS THIS, I HOPE YOU WILL THINK OF MAARTJE,
WHO LIVED IN THIS PLACE AND LOVED IT.

"Now I'm really confused," Lenni said. "What is
going on? Who are these red coats? And why does she
talk about speaking their language?"

"Can people really just come and make you move
away from your home?" Gaby asked anxiously.

They all lapsed into a gloomy silence.

THERE'S SOMETHING ELSE, Ghostwriter wrote.

51

BEGIN THY JOURNEY HERE, BESIDE THIS TREE
AND REST THY BACK AGAINST ITS ANCIENT TRUNK
THOU SHALT FEEL THE HEAT THAT USED TO BE
BEFORE OUR LUCK RAN OUT AND WE WERE SUNK.

THEN WALK STRAIGHT, AND COUNT WHAT STEPS YOU MAKE
AND TRAVEL TILL YOU COME TO THIRTY-TWO.
THEN TURN TO WHERE THE SUN SHINES WHEN YOU WAKE
AND TWENTY STEPS WILL BRING IT NEAR TO YOU.
AND NOW THY JOURNEY NEARS ITS HAPPY CLOSE.
TO THY RIGHT HAND NOW TURN THY QUEST.
YOU LISTEN WELL, AND NOW YOUR GOOD LUCK FLOWS.
NOW WALK TEN STEPS, AND THERE YOU MAKE YOUR REST.

X MARKS THE SPOT WHERE OUR FAMILY'S TREASURE LIES.
WE LEAVE IT HERE, AND WE SAY OUR GOOD-BYES.

"It's a poem," Rob said.

"It says something about a treasure!" Gaby cried. "I think this is part of Maartje's diary."

"Why are there big gaps in the lines?" Tina asked.

"I think the poem is like a map," Lenni said. "It tells us how many steps to walk, and in what direction."

"How can you tell that?" Gaby wondered.

"Look." Lenni picked up the paper and started to read. " 'Then walk straight, and count what steps you make, And travel till you come to thirty-two.' That means walk thirty-two steps. It has to mean that."

"Yeah!" Rob said. "Then it says, 'Then turn to where the sun shines when you wake.' That means turn east! Then you walk twenty steps in that direction!"

Jamal took over. " 'And now thy journey nears its happy close.' I guess 'close' means end."

"And now you're supposed to turn right," Tina said. " 'To thy right hand now turn thy quest.' What's a quest?"

"That's when you're looking for something," Alex said. "Like King Arthur and his knights were always on a quest to find something. We're on a quest to find this treasure."

"And then you walk ten steps," Tina said. They were almost at the end of the poem.

Gaby looked up from the casebook. " 'X marks the spot where our family's treasure lies. We leave it here, and we say our good-byes.' That's easy. We dig down, and there's the treasure!"

"So? What do we have?" Alex said.

Gaby showed everyone what she had written down, based on what they had figured out about the poem:

WALK THIRTY-TWO STEPS.
TURN EAST.
WALK TWENTY STEPS.
TURN RIGHT.
WALK TEN STEPS.
DIG.

"Great!" Gaby said. "We just follow these directions, and we find the treasure!"

"There's just one problem," Tina said.

Everyone turned and looked at her.

"We don't know where to start!"

"She's right," Alex said. "We didn't even look at the first part of the poem."

" 'Begin thy journey here beside this tree,' " Jamal read. "Oh, no. What tree is she talking about?"

"Let's see if we get a clue from the next few lines," Lenni said. " 'And rest thy back against its ancient trunk.' That just means lean against the tree."

" 'Thou shalt feel the heat that used to be,' " Rob read.

"Why would you feel heat from a tree?" Gaby said.

WHAT'S GOING ON? Ghostwriter flashed.

SORRY, GW, Tina wrote. WE FIGURED OUT THAT THE POEM IS A TREASURE MAP.

I SEE, Ghostwriter said.

BUT WE DON'T KNOW WHERE TO START! Jamal wrote. IS THERE ANYTHING ELSE YOU CAN FIND?

NOT IN HER HANDWRITING, Ghostwriter replied.

WELL? WHAT IS THERE THAT'S *NOT* IN HER HAND-
WRITING? Jamal wrote.

BIJBEL, Ghostwriter replied.

Bijbel? It made no sense. Tina wrote, WHAT ELSE?

Ghostwriter vanished again, and then more writing
appeared.

GEBOREN

MAARTJE VAN SALEE	6 MARTS 1653
KLAAS VAN SALEE	12 JULI 1655
WILLEM VAN SALEE	13 JANUAR 1656
ANNE VAN SALEE	9 MAJ 1658
MEINDERT VAN SALEE	19 JULI 1660
KLAAS VAN SALEE	1 JUNI 1661
WILHELMINA VAN SALEE	15 MAJ 1663

"What in the world is *Bijbel?* And *Geboren?*" Gaby
said. "They don't sound like English words."

"Well, they're sure not Spanish," Alex said. Then
he froze. "Hey, wait! They're not Spanish—but they
might be Dutch! Maartje's mother is Dutch, right?"

"Yeah!" Lenni cried.

Tina began writing. GHOSTWRITER, PLEASE GO TO
THE LIBRARY AND LOOK FOR THESE TWO WORDS.
MAYBE YOU'LL FIND THEM IN A DUTCH DICTIONARY.

Ghostwriter read what Tina wrote, then disappeared. They had to wait a long time.

Finally Ghostwriter came back.

BIJBEL = BIBLE.

GEBOREN = BIRTHS.

56

MAARTJE IS WRITING IN A DUTCH BIBLE.

"Births?" Lenni said, looking puzzled.

"Yeah—that weird list is a list of people who were born in Maartje's family," Rob said. "The numbers and words next to the names must be their birthdays."

Gaby looked at the list again. She turned pale.

"What?" Alex asked.

"Look at these dates. 1653, 1655 . . . "

"Oh, wow," Jamal breathed.

"Maartje was born in 1653—she's three hundred years old!" Tina exclaimed. "Her diary is buried under the construction site. They've been digging up *her* house!"

They all held their breath for a minute.

"That's crazy," Alex said. "Could it really be true?"

"Think about it," Rob said. "Maartje's pendant was found at the site, with all the old stuff from the house."

"And Tina and I read in the encyclopedia that Benin was famous for bronze sculpture in the 1600s," Gaby pointed out. "That must be when her father got the pendant."

"And Ghostwriter couldn't find her name in any school records," Jamal said, pointing at the page in the casebook where Gaby had written it down. "If she's three hundred years old, I guess that makes sense!"

"And remember how she talked about learning the language she was writing in? If her mother is Dutch, then English would be a foreign language to her!" Lenni burst out. She shivered. "This is kind of creepy."

"And here's the best clue of all," said Tina. "Remember how Frieda said the *English* took over the area in 1664?"

"Yes, I remember," Gaby said.

"Well, look at her diary. Maartje keeps talking about the red coats. The *Redcoats*. Get it? The Revolutionary War? The English soldiers always wore red coats!"

"Whoa," Jamal muttered.

"Well, it does make sense. But we still don't know for sure. How can we prove it?" Rob said.

"I have an idea," Gaby said. She began to write.

GHOSTWRITER! WHAT CAN YOU FIND NEAR THE DIARY?

CHEWEEZ BUBBLE GUM, Ghostwriter answered.

"That's just litter," Jamal said. "It could be anywhere."

C-7, Ghostwriter wrote. The team stared at the page. Nothing else appeared.

IS THAT A WORD? Lenni wrote.

IT'S ALL I COULD FIND.

BUT WHAT IS C-7? Gaby wrote.

I DON'T KNOW, Ghostwriter wrote.

"It might be somewhere on the site," Gaby said. "Tina and I will go down there right now."

"We're all going down there right now," Alex said. "I don't want to miss any more of this."

When the team arrived at the site ten minutes later, the table of artifacts was covered with strange objects.

"Where have you guys been?" Jasmine yelled,

58

bounding toward them. "Hi, Jamal," she added, blushing a little. Jamal smiled back at her.

"I know what I want to do!" Jasmine was chattering excitedly. "I'm going to college to study archaeology! I had no idea how much you could find out by digging stuff up from the ground. Wait till you see what we found!"

"Jasmine—" Tina began.

"Come over here!" Jasmine was still talking, too excited to listen. "I've been working on section E-8. That's in the middle of the house. There was a fireplace, and two rooms, one on either side of the fireplace." She showed them where a rusted metal plate was sticking up from the ground in a ditch. "That's the back of the fireplace," she said. "And do you see this extra wall? That was where the people slept. Their beds were built into the wall!"

"This is section E-8?" Lenni said.

"Yeah! There's a team assigned to each section," Jasmine said. Gaby and Tina looked at each other.

"Is there a section C-7?" Tina asked.

"Uh-huh. Over here." Jasmine led them to another section, where two people from the projects were working with Frieda. "This is C-7. Why did you want to know?"

"Well—um—" Gaby tried to sound casual. "You didn't find, like, a book or something here, did you?"

Jasmine shrugged. "Frieda? Did we find a book here?"

Frieda looked up and straightened the bandanna on

her head. "No, a book wouldn't survive being buried here."

Tina squeezed Gaby's hand. "It's not here."

Gaby looked at her. Tina's eyes shone with tears.

"Can we see what you *did* find?" Gaby asked.

"Sure," Jasmine said. The team followed her to the long table. It was covered with artifacts and separated into the different grid numbers.

"Let's see." Jasmine counted them off. "This is the stuff from C-5. Here's C-6 . . . Aha! C-7. What are you looking for?"

"We're not sure," Gaby said. "We just had a hunch, and we want to check it out." They looked at the things on the table. There wasn't much.

"This stuff came from outside the house," Jasmine began telling them. "This is part of an old horse bridle." She pointed at a metal ring. "And this is a nail."

"What's in that box?" Lenni said. The box sat at the edge of the table. It was about the size of a foot-locker, and completely rusted. It was fastened with an old, rotten leather strap. Gaby touched the box.

"Eeew," she said. "It's all crusty."

"We don't know what's in there yet," Jasmine said.

"But you've got to open it!" Tina said frantically.

"You never know," Gaby said. "There could be something in there that might, I don't know, tell you where something else might be buried."

"Like what?" Jasmine asked, squinting at Gaby.

"I don't know. Like, uh, a treasure," Gaby said.

"A treasure!" Jasmine laughed. "Gaby, you're a

trip. You'll have a better chance of finding a treasure if you join in and start digging. We only have one more day, and we're not even halfway done!"

"Jasmine, *please*," Tina said.

Jasmine stopped talking and looked curiously at Tina.

"It kind of means a lot to her," Alex added. "To all of us, actually."

"Okay. I'll tell Frieda and Ted." Jasmine ran to call the two graduate students over.

"What's going on?" Ted asked when they were all gathered in front of the box.

Jasmine shot a look at Tina and Gaby. "There might be something in there that could tell us about the site. Then we would know where to look and what to look for!"

Frieda sighed. "I wanted to take it to a lab, but since it's not airtight, I don't think we'll be messing with it too much." She walked around the table to the box. Tina was almost squeezing Gaby's hand off.

Frieda began fiddling with the box. She used long metal instruments to gently push aside the rotted leather. It fell away, and finally she got the latch open. She swung the top of the box open. Then she gasped.

A huge book, stamped BIJBEL, sat inside the box.

Chapter

8

"How did this ever survive?" Frieda asked.

"Open it," Tina said. Frieda carefully opened the book, and everyone crowded around. Many of the pages were eaten away or too rotten to handle. But they could make out some odd, spiky handwriting in the margins.

"Someone was keeping a journal here," Ted said. He and Frieda leaned close to the paper. "It's written in English," he added. "That's odd."

"It was a girl named Maartje," Frieda said after a while. She pronounced it MAR-ee-tee.

"She was eleven, and her family lived in this house," Frieda went on, peering at the big book. "Her father taught her English." She turned a few more pages, and saw the record of births. "Big family," she commented.

As she flipped the pages, a piece of parchment paper fell out of the Bible. Gaby dove for it. It was the poem that Ghostwriter had shown the team, but there was a strange, delicate drawing of a tree where Ghostwriter had only seen a big space.

"It's a poem," Frieda said.

"It's a map," Ted said.

"It's a picture of a tree," Jasmine said.

"It's all three," Gaby said. "Read it!"

It didn't take Frieda and Ted too long to figure out exactly what the Ghostwriter Team had figured out.

"So we just have to start at a tree," Jasmine said.

"Hold it," Frieda said. "Which tree? Any trees that were here then are long gone now."

"Oh, no," Tina said.

"Wait!" Jasmine shouted. "I knew that tree looked familiar. Come here!" She ran over to the section she had been working on and pointed at the metal rectangle.

"That used to be the fireplace," she said. "They used metal as the back of the fireplace. Look closely at it."

Frieda, Ted, and the Ghostwriter Team crowded around. They could see a faint picture of a beautiful, ornate tree on the blackened metal.

"This is the tree," Jasmine said. "This is the tree that they meant!"

"That's why the poem talks about 'the heat that used to be'!" Gaby shouted. "It's part of the fireplace!"

"Great!" Ted clapped his hands. "Now let's find whatever we're supposed to find."

"Tina," Frieda said. "Maartje was about your age, and she was probably about your size. We'd better use you as our measuring guide. Her steps were probably

the same size as yours. Put your back against the tree. There. Now—what does the poem say?"

" 'Then walk straight, and count what steps you make, and travel till you come to thirty-two,' " Gaby read.

"So you walk thirty-two steps."

They all counted together as they followed Tina along. The other diggers began looking on curiously.

"Now 'turn to where the sun shines when you wake,' " Frieda coached. "That's east. All right, now 'twenty steps will bring it near to you.' Walk twenty steps." The group following Tina became larger. Everyone was silent.

"Okay. 'To thy right hand now turn thy quest.' Turn right," Frieda said. "Then 'walk ten steps.' " Everyone counted out loud. " 'And there you make your rest.' "

They found themselves outside the roped-off area.

"We weren't even planning to dig here," Ted said.

"Maybe our plans were wrong," Frieda said, shrugging.

They had to dig very carefully, in case anything else was buried there. It took a long time. All the volunteer diggers stood around and watched.

Suddenly they hit something hard and couldn't dig any farther. Ted jumped into the hole with a brush and began whisking the dirt away.

"This seems to be the front of the house," he said. "These are tiles that were placed around the front door." As he carefully brushed the dirt away, the kids saw that the tiles were arranged in an intricate pattern.

"Well? What now?" Frieda asked him.

Tina looked at the tiles, then at the map. Suddenly the X in the last line began to glow. Ghostwriter was trying to tell her something!

She held her breath. The X flew off the page, then moved into the hole and rested on the tiles. When it disappeared, Tina could clearly see—some of the tiles in the pattern made a big letter X!

"I know!" she said, jumping into the hole. "Look." She traced her finger along the tiles Ghostwriter had shown her. "X marks the spot!"

"Amazing," Frieda said. "X actually marks the spot!"

Slowly and painstakingly, Frieda and Ted began prying up the tiles.

"These tiles are valuable, even if there *isn't* treasure buried beneath them," Ted explained.

"It's taking so long!" Gaby complained. "I could never be an archaeologist! Everything goes so slowly."

"You're not exactly the patient type," said Alex. Gaby stuck her tongue out at him.

"But look at what we did here in just one weekend," Frieda said, her eyes still on her work. "Look at everything you guys did!"

Gaby looked around the construction site. It *was* amazing. Working together, the people of the neighborhood had turned a vacant lot into a sort of museum. . . . She saw Mr. Barrett standing near the table, and was about to point him out to Tina, when Ted shouted, "Here it is!"

Gaby leaned over as far as she could to watch Ted and Frieda drag another box out of the hole beneath the tiles.

Everyone from the site, all the volunteers, crowded around as Ted opened the box. The lid opened with a creak.

Inside, something metal glinted.

"Is it gold?" one man asked.

"Maybe this guy was a pirate!" an old woman said.

"What is it?" a boy said.

Frieda and Ted studied the contents of the box.

"It's not gold," Frieda finally said. "It's brass."

Everyone moved back, disappointed.

"Wait. That doesn't mean it's not valuable," said Ted. Everyone leaned forward again.

"Look at this stuff," Ted said. He held up a brass bell. It was carved with the same symbols as the little head Jasmine had found. "This is from the Bight of Benin." He held up another piece. It looked like a dog. "This, too." He held up each piece, getting more and more excited.

"This is the most amazing collection of brass figures I've ever seen. There's a whole museum-full of these here! This is worth more than gold."

"It's all Papa Salee had from his life in Africa," Frieda said, touching the yellow metal.

"Here's our proof. This site *is* special," Ted said,

looking at Frieda. "An African settled on this farm. He was one of the first African Americans!"

"That's right," Frieda said, picking up the Bible. "It says in here that Maartje's father was African, and her mother was a white Dutch woman. This was one of the first African American settlements in Brooklyn. We can figure out how they lived from day to day, this farmer and his family."

Everyone crowded around to get a closer look.

It was starting to get dark. Tina looked around her. She squinted her eyes and everything got a little blurry. The lamppost sort of looked like a big tree. A taxi stopped short at a light, squeaking its brakes. For a second, it almost sounded like a horse neighing. Tina looked around some more. She could see the foundations of the house, where they had been dug up. The walls would have been right there. The fire would be blazing inside, in the fireplace decorated with the tree. Maartje would be sitting in front of it, braiding her sister's hair while their mother sang Dutch songs to them and their father told them stories of Africa. But outside there would be something moving in the dark. . . .

"Hey! Something's moving over there!" Tina yelled. Everyone looked at her, then at where she was pointing.

"It's one of the bulldozers!" Jasmine gasped.

The machine began rolling slowly across the lot. In another few seconds, it would begin plowing through the remains of the house.

"Everyone move back!" Frieda yelled.

"*Alex*!" Gaby screamed.

Everyone looked in horror where Gaby was pointing. Alex was standing near the foundations of the house. When he heard his name being called, he turned around and saw the bulldozer coming straight at him. He leaped backward. But one of ropes caught his foot and he fell flat on the ground. He was about to be run over!

But Ted was already running across the lot, yelling and waving his arms. The bulldozer kept moving. He grabbed on to the back of it. They all held their breath. Just when it looked as if he would be crushed by the huge rolling wheels, he swung himself into the control cabin and pulled one of the levers. The machine shuddered and stopped with a clang.

Everyone cheered and ran toward Alex, who collapsed in an exhausted heap on a big pile of dirt.

"Are you okay?" Gaby asked. Alex opened his eyes.

"I'm fine," he said. But when he tried to stand up, his knees were shaking so badly, he had to sit down again.

"Maybe you're not quite *fine*," Jamal pointed out. "That was a close call."

"Yeah," Alex said. He looked up at Ted, who had turned off the engine and was climbing down. "Thanks. You saved my life."

"I'm just glad you're okay," Ted said.

"You must have been scared," Jasmine said to him.

"I don't know. I sure am now!" Ted laughed. His face was red and he was sweating. He helped Alex up.

"The gas pedal got wedged down somehow," Ted explained. "It was running blind."

Jamal frowned. "How could that happen?"

"I don't know," Ted said, looking puzzled. "I'll tell Barrett he should have that machine checked."

Everyone began walking back toward the artifacts table. Then they all stopped short.

"Where—where's all the stuff?" Gaby said.

The long table that had held everything they found in the old farmhouse was still filled with small artifacts. But the Bible, the map, and the African bronze pieces were gone!

Chapter

9

"Oh, no! Oh, no!" Frieda moaned. "We need that stuff to show to the people from OHP. They won't let us keep working if we can't prove that someone important lived here!"

Lenni pointed at the table. "The Bible was right here," she said. "You can see the outlines in the dirt."

"Maybe this place is haunted!" an old man said. "That old farmer doesn't like us digging up all his things. He got mad and took them back!"

"Gramp," a boy said, "there's no such thing as ghosts."

"If there were ghosts, I think they'd be glad to be remembered," Tina said, thinking of Ghostwriter.

"I can't believe this. This is horrible! Ted, call the police. Somebody help me look," Frieda said, running to each of the large holes around the site.

Gaby grabbed Tina's arm, whipping her around.

"Ow!" Tina exclaimed. "What's up, Gaby?"

"I think the stuff was stolen!" Gaby whispered.

Tina looked at the other members of the team. They all gathered together, and Jasmine joined them. The volunteers swarmed around, looking for the missing artifacts.

"But who would steal this stuff?" Jamal asked. "It's only worth a lot to us, because we want to study it."

"It wasn't stolen for the money. It was stolen to stop us from digging here," Gaby said.

"Gaby, what are you talking about?" Alex said.

"Mr. Barrett stole everything to keep us from finding stuff here," Gaby said. "He said he'd *make sure* we didn't find anything. Didn't he?" She looked at Tina.

"Oh, Gaby," Jasmine said. "He was just talking." Then she thought for a second. "Wasn't he?" she asked.

"Maybe Gaby's right," Jamal said. "The way that bulldozer took off by itself was pretty suspicious. Maybe Barrett arranged that to distract us while he stole the stuff from the table."

"Yeah!" Gaby cried. "Come on, let's sneak a look in his trailer!"

"No way, Gaby," Alex said firmly. "I had a really close call back there. If this guy Barrett is the one who nearly ran me over, he's dangerous. No way are you going to poke around in his trailer. Especially not at night. We'll look for proof tomorrow."

"Okay, people," Frieda shouted. Everyone turned and looked at her. She was standing in the middle of the lot.

"Let's call it a night," she said in a weary voice.

73

"We've searched high and low. The stuff is gone. Maybe the police will be able to track it down, but there's nothing more we can do now." Her shoulders slumped. "Maybe we should just give this project up."

"But we can't give up now," Jasmine cried.

"I didn't know there were African Americans here so long ago," a woman said. "And I definitely didn't know there were *free* African Americans here. We wouldn't have known that if it weren't for this project."

"If we can't find the things we found already, we'll just find some more things," the old man spoke up. "As long as it isn't that old farmer haunting us, I'll keep coming back here to help."

"Me too," said his grandson.

All the volunteers began saying they would come back and look for more artifacts. Finally Frieda smiled.

"Okay! I won't quit if you won't." She looked around. "We'll meet back here tomorrow."

The next morning, the site was bustling. Everyone had brought friends to help. The news was all over the neighborhood.

Tina and Gaby got there bright and early. The rest of the team was going to meet them after a rehearsal for the spring show. "There are so many more people here today!" Tina said, taping different parts of the site.

Then Tina spotted Mr. Barrett out there, digging with a group of volunteers. She nudged Gaby. "Look, Mr. Barrett's even helping. Gaby, maybe you were wrong about him."

Gaby took the camera from Tina's hands and handed it to Jasmine.

"Hey!" Tina said.

"Jasmine, you tape for a while. Get shots of people digging and stuff. Tina and I have to do something."

"Oh, Gaby, remember what your brother said about doing dangerous things . . ." Jasmine warned.

"I know! I wanted to do this last night, and I didn't because it was too dangerous. We're just going to look around a little."

"Okay, okay. But be careful," Jasmine said.

"I'm always careful!" Gaby replied.

"What are we going to do?" Tina asked as Gaby pulled her away.

"I'm not sure," Gaby said. They walked over to Mr. Barrett's trailer. "I just know the stuff is in there somewhere."

"But we were in there," Tina protested. "Remember? There's no place in there for him to hide anything."

"But there must have been someplace," Gaby said. "He would have had to hide it in a hurry, and if he had a car or something, we would have heard it take off. The stuff has to be on the site somewhere."

Tina sighed as Gaby led her around the back of the trailer. "This is how we listened in," Gaby said. "Remember? Now let me climb on your shoulders again."

Tina wasn't scared this time. "What are you going to listen for? He's not even in there."

But Gaby was busy doing something to the vent. Tina couldn't see because Gaby's legs on her shoulders

75

blocked her vision. She heard something thump on the ground next to her. Then Gaby wasn't there anymore. She looked around.

"Gaby?" she said. Next to her, she saw the metal grille that had been over the vent. She looked up in time to see Gaby's legs vanish into the trailer.

"Gaby!" she whispered loudly. "What are you doing?"

"Relax," Gaby called from inside the trailer. "I'm just looking around. I just remembered. Mr. Barrett had hardly any furniture in here, but he did have that big closet that looked like it was part of the wall."

Tina called back, "Gaby, please come back out!"

"Whoa!" Tina heard a creak from inside.

"Tina, I found it! All the missing stuff is right in here! In the built-in closet!"

Suddenly Tina heard another noise. Someone was walking toward the trailer. She peeked around the side, and saw Mr. Barrett walking toward her. He didn't see her.

"Gaby," she called in a hoarse whisper. "Mr. Barrett's here! Get out of there!" She heard something creak again.

But Mr. Barrett's keys were already jangling in the lock. Tina heard the door open, and expected to hear him shout at Gaby. But she didn't hear anything. There were no shouts, no slams, no sounds of a struggle. Mr. Barrett just seemed to be going about his business.

Tina knew Gaby was in there somewhere. But where? And how was she going to get out?

Chapter
10

At that moment, Tina saw Alex, Jamal, Lenni, and Rob walking onto the site. She ran over to them.

"Gaby's in trouble," she said. "She was in Mr. Barrett's trailer—she climbed in the vent—and all the stuff was in there—but then he came in—but I don't know where she went—"

"You mean she's in there now?" Alex said.

"Yes! But Mr. Barrett doesn't know she's in there."

"What are we going to do?" Lenni asked. "He wouldn't hurt her, would he?"

"Look!" Rob cried. He pointed over Tina's shoulder.

A sign behind Tina said BARRETT CONSTRUCTION COMPANY, but the letters "S and O" were lighting up one by one, over and over again in a pattern that spelled SOS. They all looked at each other. Gaby must have contacted Ghostwriter!

The members of the team moved closer together, and Rob dragged an old page from a newspaper toward them with his foot. They all looked down at it. Immediately the words on the dirty newspaper page began rearranging. A message from Gaby appeared.

GHOSTWRITER, GET HELP! I'M IN THE BUILT-IN CLOSET. MR. BARRETT IS WALKING AROUND. HE DOESN'T KNOW I'M IN HERE. BUT I HEARD HIM ON THE PHONE, AND HE'S PLANNING TO DESTROY ALL THIS STUFF!

Tina opened her notebook and uncapped the pen that hung around her neck.

PLEASE TELL GABY NOT TO WORRY, she wrote. WE'RE COMING UP WITH A PLAN.

HURRY UP, the message came back. IF HE OPENS THE CLOSET, I'M IN BIG TROUBLE!!

"Maybe we should just go confront him," Alex said.

"Yeah, *right*," Tina said. "He doesn't care about a bunch of kids. He said so. We have to find someone he'd be scared of, and then get that person to go to his trailer."

They heard voices behind them, and they all turned around. Mr. Cruz was standing with Frieda, Ted, and Jasmine. Ted was holding the few things they had found that day—two old pipe stems and a spoon—and Frieda was talking and waving her arms. The team walked over to them.

"I'm sorry," Mr. Cruz was saying. "This just isn't enough. We'll have to let them start building tomorrow."

Just then Mr. Barrett came out of his trailer, locking the door behind him. He had a big fake smile on his face. He walked over to the group.

78

"But we found a lot of old stuff before!" Jasmine protested. "It got stolen last night."

Mr. Barrett shook his head. "You found a few pieces of junk. Who says it was even really that old?"

"There was an old Bible," Frieda said. "In it there was evidence that this was a farmhouse—and that a free African American family lived here!"

"Oh, come on," Mr. Barrett scoffed. "A farmhouse, *here*? You people are really too much. I don't know why Shop-Mart wants to build a supermarket in this neighborhood. You can't even turn your back for five seconds without all your stuff getting stolen off a table!"

"We live here," Jasmine said angrily. "And this neighborhood has *history*!"

Tina's mind was racing. "Mr. Barrett, how did you know the stuff got stolen off a table while our backs were turned?" Everyone looked at her. "You weren't here. How would you know that?"

Mr. Barrett crossed his arms. "Do I have to listen to this kid?" he growled.

"Oh, yes, you do," Tina said. She couldn't believe she was talking this way. But thinking of Gaby locked in the closet made her feel brave. "You do have to listen to this. Gaby found the Bible and the other stuff in your trailer, in the built-in closet. She climbed in a window, and she got stuck inside. She's there right now!"

"That's a serious charge," Mr. Cruz said. "Barrett? Is this true?"

"They're crazy!" he said. "Are you going to listen to a bunch of kids from the projects?"

79

"I grew up in the projects," Mr. Cruz said, and began walking to the trailer. Mr. Barrett followed him.

"Wait—" he said. "I didn't mean— There's no stuff in there— Well, if there is, someone planted it!"

"The keys?" Mr. Cruz said. Mr. Barrett handed them over, looking sick.

Mr. Cruz stepped into the trailer, followed closely by Mr. Barrett. Mr. Cruz opened the built-in closet.

"I was just trying to keep the stuff safe," Mr. Barrett said. "I thought it would be safe in here."

Gaby stepped out triumphantly and handed Mr. Cruz the Bible.

"Were you trying to keep Gaby safe, too?" Mr. Cruz asked sternly.

Tina walked slowly home from Gaby and Alex's house. The team had met there to discuss the exciting events of the weekend. Tina had forgotten all about Tuan and her father.

But now here she was, outside her apartment door. She took a deep breath and let it out. She knew what to expect at home now. Everyone would be angry at everyone else, and no one would be talking.

"Tina!" her father said when she came inside. "I'm glad you are finally here. Welcome to our new home!"

"Huh?" Tina stared. Her mother was sitting at the kitchen table, smiling. Tuan looked slightly confused. Linda came running into the room, giggling.

"I put up Father's sign!" she said.

"What sign?" Tina asked. She wasn't sure what was

80

going on. Had everyone gone crazy while she was out?

"Come and look," Mrs. Nguyen said. "Your father is changing his mind a little." They all went down the hallway to the living room. A beautiful carved wooden screen had been put up in the middle of the room. On the screen, Tina saw the sign her father had made.

TUAN'S BACHELOR PAD. ALL-AMERICAN.

"Bachelor pad?" Tina said. "What does that mean?"

"I saw it on that show on TV, the one with the two men who share an apartment and they are driving each other crazy," Mr. Nguyen said.

"You mean *The Odd Couple?*" Tina asked.

"Yes! They talked about their bachelor pad." Mr. Nguyen looked at Tuan. "We are in America now. I don't want to make you angry at the Vietnamese part of you, so maybe I will let a little more of America into my house."

"I like it," Tuan said after a moment.

"I am glad to hear that," his father said.

"Anyway," Tuan went on, "that apartment was a mess, with all those guys living there. And it was too much money!" He turned to Mrs. Nguyen. "And none of them know how to make good noodles. Only Italian spaghetti." He looked at his father. His ears were red. "I'm sorry, Father," he said in a low voice.

"There's something I want to say to you, Tuan," Mrs. Nguyen said. The family turned to look at her.

"It is very nice that your father has given you an

All-American Bachelor Pad and that he is letting in some more of America to this house. But Vietnam is very important to him. To me, too. You keep telling us that you are grown up now. If this is true, then you must try to understand both sides of the problem. Your father is acting very American for you, but his heart is Vietnamese. Please don't make him bend too far in your direction."

Tuan was quiet for a minute. Then he took a Magic Marker from Linda. He crossed off the ALL from ALL-AMERICAN and wrote PART. They looked at the sign.

TUAN'S BACHELOR PAD, it said. PART-AMERICAN.

A few weeks later the team, Jasmine, Frieda, and Ted met at the Youth Center. Their families were there, too, as well as a crowd of people from the projects. A long table was piled with food, but no one was eating. They were all watching Gaby on a big TV screen.

"All the stuff from the dig will be put in the Museum of the City of New York," she was saying. "It's a piece of New York history, right here for everyone to see. And the brass sculptures will be put in their own display in the Brooklyn Museum's collection of African art. And, in case you were wondering, Mr. Barrett is out of business and behind bars."

The camera focused in on the little bronze pendant that Jasmine had found. Everyone clapped as the image faded. Then the mayor of New York came on the screen.

"That was the winning entry in our history contest," he said. "It was made by Gabriela Fernandez, Jasmine Morton, and Tina Nguyen, three students from Fort Greene, Brooklyn. I congratulate these students, and thank them for showing us just how much history New York has to offer."

Everyone clapped again as the commercials came on.

"I'm very proud of you children," Gaby's mother said. "You really did a great thing."

"Well, if Frieda and Ted hadn't started the dig, we wouldn't have known what to do for the contest," Gaby said.

"Hey, Gaby, if you hadn't wanted to poke around the site, we never would have found Maartje's pendant," Jasmine put in. "And we might never have run into Mr. Barrett and gotten suspicious of him."

"Me and my great ideas," Gaby said, grinning.

Frieda put an arm around Gaby. "I'm just glad everything came out all right," she said.

"I keep thinking about Maartje," Tina said. "In a way, I feel like she's my friend. I wonder what happened to her? Like, did her family find a place to live? Did everything turn out all right?"

"That's the thing about archaeology," Ted said. "You find out pieces of stories, but then you have to fill in the blanks. Maybe we can find the answers in old archives or family records. But we might never know."

"That's so frustrating," Jasmine said.

"Still want to study archaeology?" Frieda asked her.

"Yes! I'd rather know some stuff than nothing at all!" Jasmine said hastily. "It's not *that* frustrating!"

Gaby caught Tina's eye and pointed at the big banner over the door. CONGRATULATIONS, it said. Ghostwriter was making it blink on and off, like Christmas lights.

"He's glad we found the farmhouse," Gaby whispered. "That way Maartje won't be forgotten."

"It's funny," Tina said softly. "We know more about Maartje than we do about Ghostwriter. Maybe someday we'll find out who he is, and where he came from, too."

"Hey, Tina?" Gaby said after a second.

"What?"

"I have a *great* idea!"

"Uh-oh," Tina said. "Here we go again!"

WATCH IT! SOLVE IT! TELL A FRIEND!

It's the team's first adventure! Strange creatures, backpack robberies and a secret code!

Ghostwriter Is Now Available On Videocassette!

$14.98* EACH
*Suggested Retail Price

FREE! Cool *Ghostwriter* Puzzles inside each cassette!